WHO GOT THE BABY IN THE KING CAKE?

Written and Illustrated
by JOHNETTE DOWNING

To Natalie.
You got the
— baby!

Johnette Downing

RIVER ROAD PRESS

New Orleans 2019

ISBN: 978-1-941879-24-5

The name and logo for "River Road Press" are trademarks of River Road Press LLC and are registered with the U.S. Patent and Trademark Office.

For information regarding permission to reproduce selections from this book, write to Permissions, River Road Press LLC, P.O. Box 125, Metairie, Louisiana 70001.

For information on other River Road Press titles, please visit www.riverroadpress.com.

Printed in Korea

Published by River Road Press
P.O. Box 125
Metairie, LA 70001

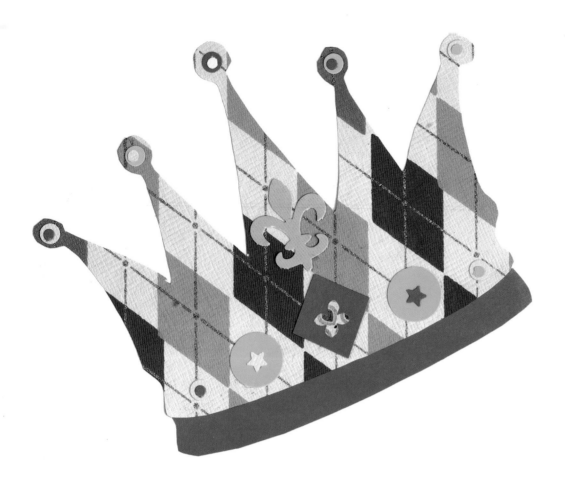

Roll out the dough to make a **KING CAKE.**

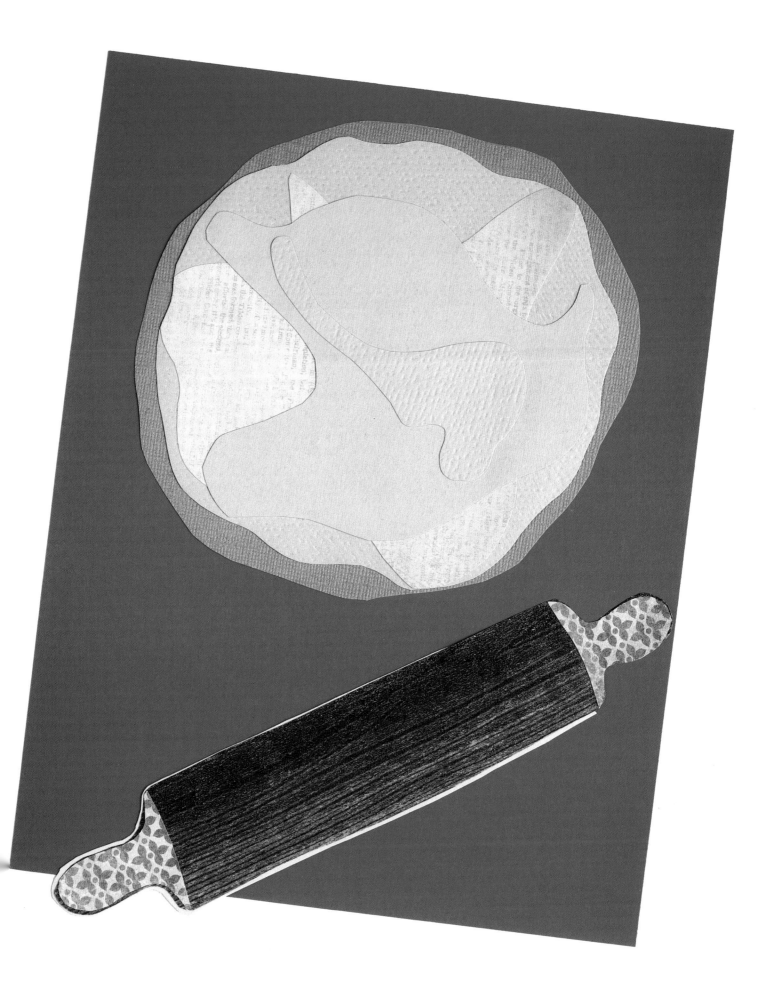

Spread a little filling in the **KING CAKE**.

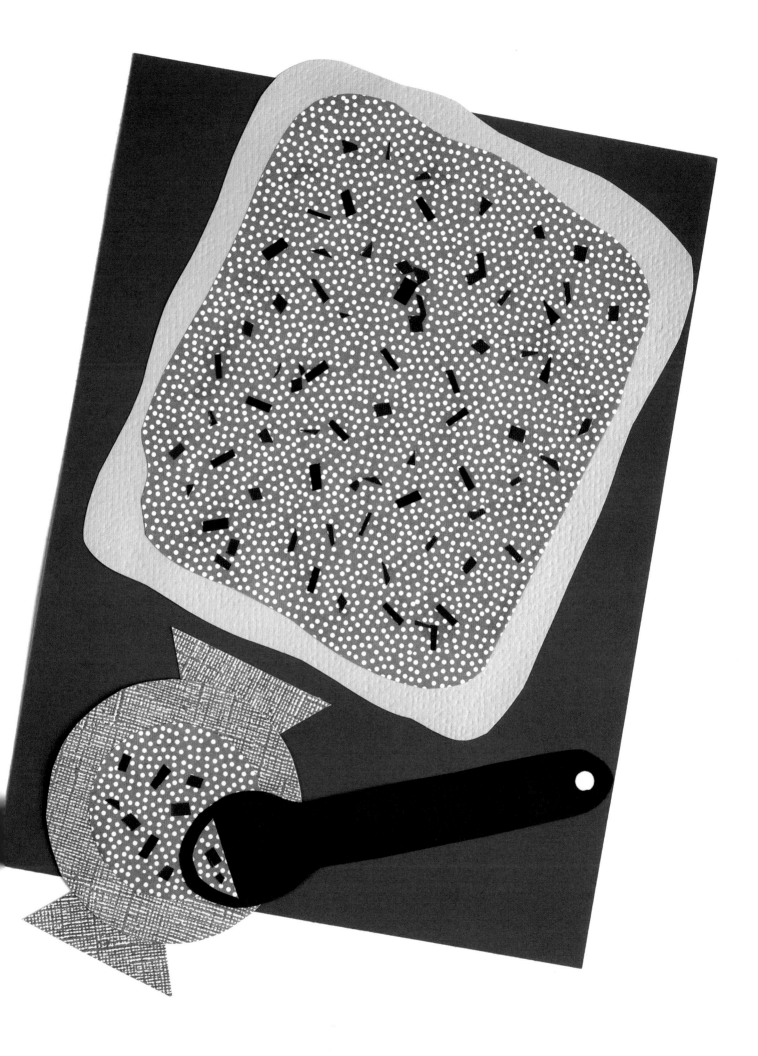

Braid it in a circle for a

KING CAKE.

Into the oven

goes the **KING CAKE**.

Then you take the cake out of the **OVEN.**

When it cools down you add a little **ICING.**

Sprinkle colored sugar for a **TOPPING**.

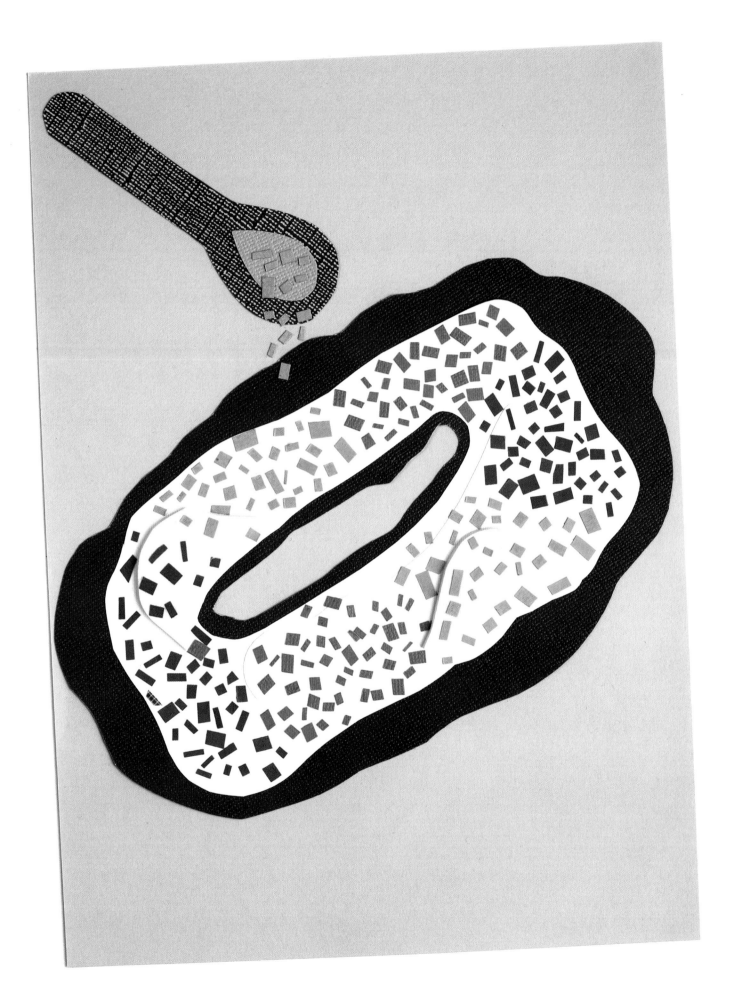

Hide a plastic baby in the

KING CAKE.

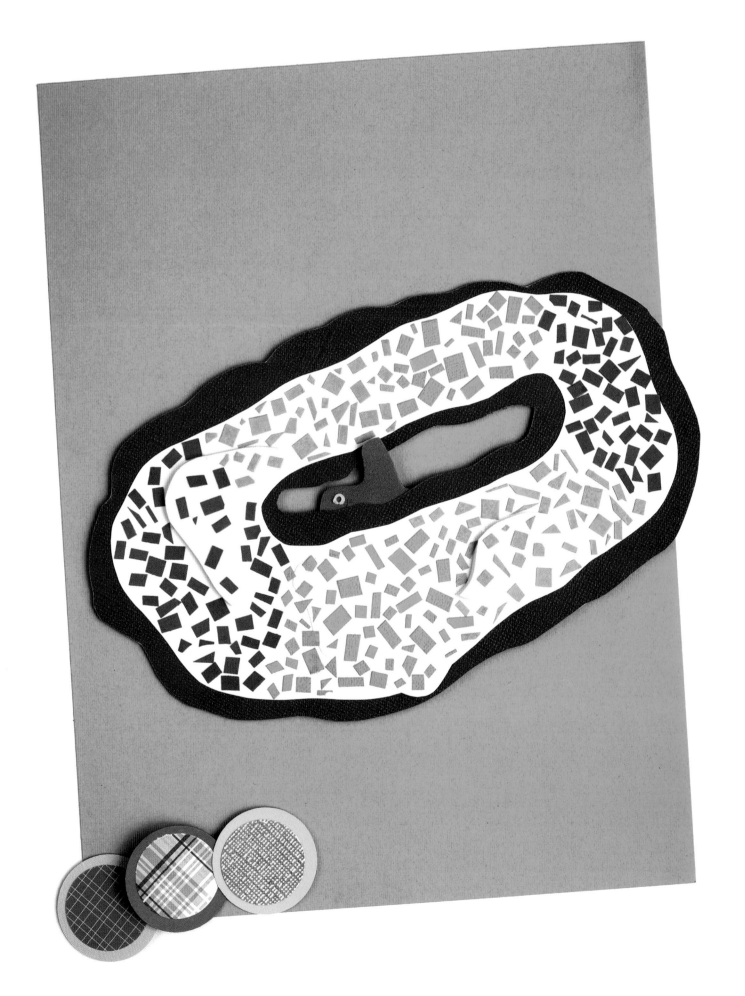

Let's party! It's **MARDI GRAS**

way down in NEW ORLEANS.

Let's party! It's **CARNIVAL!**

If you bring the RICE, I'll bring the BEANS.

Who got the baby in the KING CAKE?

Did she find the baby in the KING CAKE?

Did he get the baby in the KING CAKE?

What happens when you get the **BABY**?
You have to give the next **PARTY**.

Invite all your friends and your FAMILY

to eat king cake and be MERRY!

Let's party! It's MARDI GRAS way down in NEW ORLEANS.

Let's party! It's CARNIVAL.

If you bring the RICE,

I'll bring the BEANS.

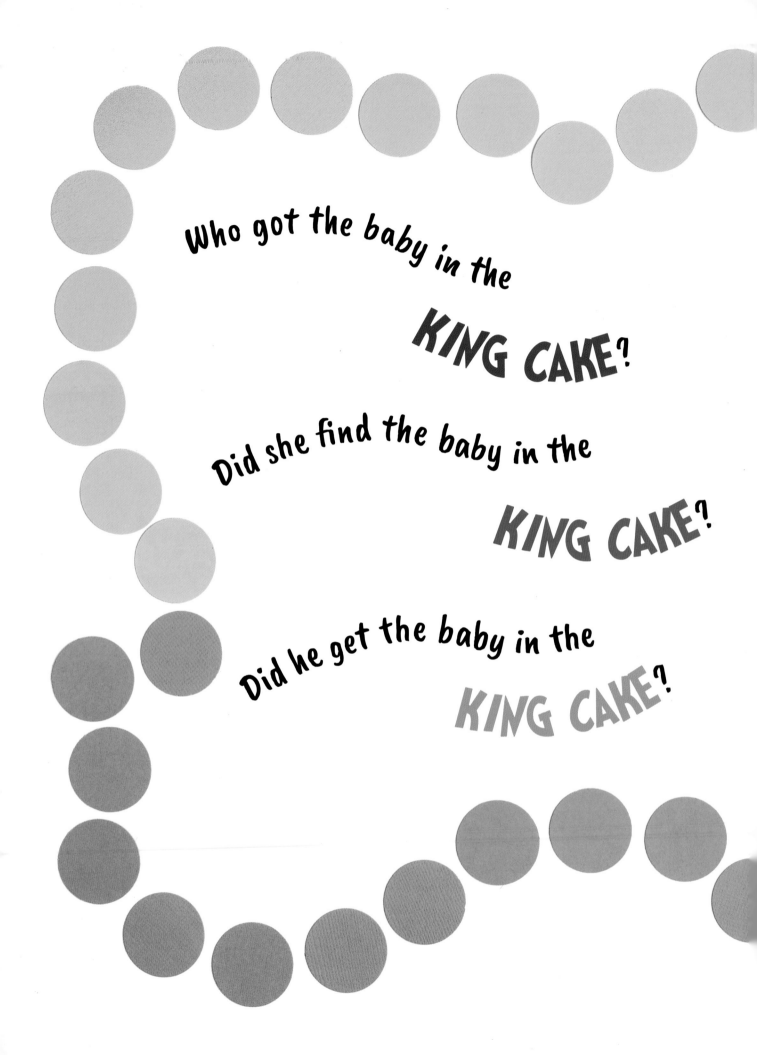

Who got the baby in the **KING CAKE?**

Did she find the baby in the **KING CAKE?**

Did he get the baby in the **KING CAKE?**

AUTHOR'S NOTE

As part of a Roman Catholic custom, the coming of the three wise men bearing gifts to the Christ child is celebrated in New Orleans each year on January 6. Referred to as Twelfth Night, the Feast of the Epiphany, or Epiphany, this celebration marks the beginning of Carnival season. Over the next several weeks of merriment, anticipation builds until the season ends on Fat Tuesday, known in Louisiana as Mardi Gras, the day before Ash Wednesday. It is a time for feasting and gift giving before the fasting and religious observance of Lent. The culinary centerpiece of this season is the sharing of king cake.

Believed to have originated nearly a thousand years ago in France, the cake is an *homage* to the wise men or the three kings. The cake is braided into a round shape, covered in icing, and sprinkled generously with sugar in the Mardi Gras colors of green, gold, and purple. Green represents faith, gold represents power, and purple represents justice. The cake's circular shape resembles a king's crown, but in New Orleans, the cake is typically oblong. Some say the cake is round to resemble the route the three kings took to Bethlehem. Many king cakes are flavored with cinnamon, while others have cream or fruit fillings.

In Europe and beyond, a bean, pea, pecan, or coin is hidden inside the cake. In New Orleans, it is a plastic king cake baby, which, as Mardi Gras historian Arthur Hardy notes, was introduced by McKenzie's Bakery as a replacement for a more expensive porcelain doll. While some have claimed an association with the baby Jesus, it may be more representative of a New Year's baby. The lucky person who finds the baby in their piece of king cake is unofficially crowned king or queen for the day and is expected to host the next king cake party as a way of spreading good fortune and ensuring that the festivities continue throughout the Carnival season. At king cake parties, where favorite dishes such as red beans and rice are also served, you will hear locals ask, "Who got the baby in the king cake?" This question is the inspiration for this book.

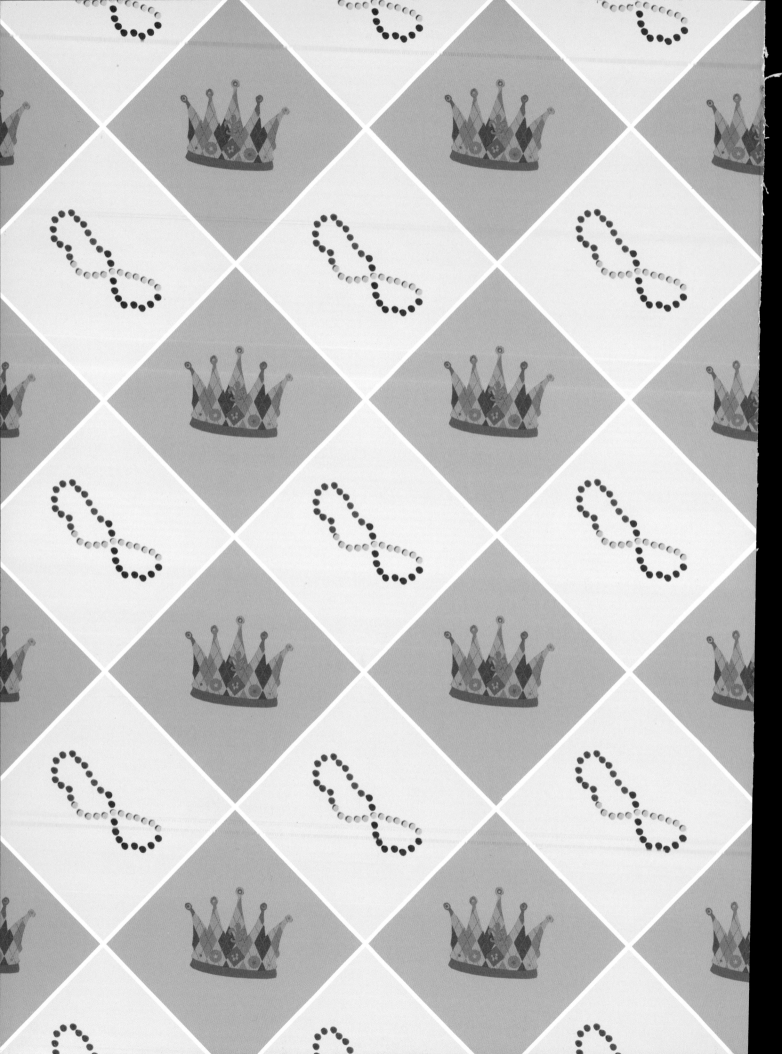